# BOYS
## CAMP

# ZEE'S STORY
# BOYS CAMP

Written by Kitson Jazynka and Valerie Tripp
Illustrated by Craig Orback

**Every boy has
a great story.**

Sky Pony Press
New York

Sky Pony Press books may be purchased in bulk at special discounts for sales promotion, corporate gifts, fund-raising, or educational purposes. Special editions can also be created to specifications. For details, contact the Special Sales Department, Sky Pony Press, 307 West 36th Street, 11th Floor, New York, NY 10018 or info@skyhorsepublishing.com.

Sky Pony® is a registered trademark of Skyhorse Publishing, Inc.®, a Delaware corporation.

Visit our website at www.skyponypress.com.

10 9 8 7 6 5 4 3 2 1

Manufactured in China, January 2015
This product conforms to CPSIA 2008

Library of Congress Cataloging-in-Publication Data

Jazynka, Kitson, author.
  Zee's story / written by Kitson Jazynka and Valerie Tripp ; illustrated by Craig Orback.
    pages cm. — (Boys camp ; # 3)
  Summary: "Zee must face his scariest, most dangerous crisis on his own while on a kayaking trip, and for a while, it looks like all is lost. One thing's for sure: Zee will have an adventure-packed summer at Camp Wolf Trail!"— Provided by publisher.
  ISBN 978-1-62914-754-3 (hc : alk. paper)
  [1. Camps—Fiction. 2. Kayaks and kayaking—Fiction.] I. Tripp, Valerie, 1951- author. II. Orback, Craig, illustrator. III. Title.
  PZ7.J353Ze 2015
  [Fic]—dc23
                    2014041529

Cover design by Brian Peterson
Cover illustration credit Craig Orback

Kayaking card illustrations by Ryan Martinez

Ebook ISBN: 978-1-63220-817-0

Have fun. Make friends. Be yourself.

Hello, Camper!

All of us at Camp Wolf Trail are looking forward to greeting you on July 10. We've got a great summer ahead of us.

Pretty soon you'll be packing your trunk for your two weeks here at camp. If this is your first summer at Wolf Trail, you're probably curious—and maybe even a little nervous—about what to expect, especially if this is your first time away from home.

Well, first of all, don't worry. Camp is fun. And here at Wolf Trail, we've been sharing the fun with kids like you for more than fifty years.

As soon as you arrive, counselors and returning campers will welcome you and help you find the way to your cabin. The cabins are are scattered like acorns throughout the woods. You'll be sharing your cabin with eight other campers and two counselors.

Counselors and campers of different ages are assigned to groups called "clusters." Together, you and your cluster will come up with a funny name and a signature move for your group. You'll take turns doing communal chores, like setting the table for eighty hungry monkeys (also known as the campers, counselors, and camp staff). You and your cluster will compete against other clusters during our camp theme days, including the Oddball Championships. Past themes have been Martian Day, Rock Star Day, Backwards Day, Half Magic Day, and Chicken-of-the-Woods Day.

*Every* day there are lots of activities to choose from: swimming in clear, cool Evergreen Lake, boating, canoeing, arts and crafts, hiking, sports, and trail blazing (also known as bushwhacking). At night everyone at camp gathers around a fire for songs, stories, jokes, and reflection. And each week you and your fellow campers and counselors will go off on a wilderness adventure into the woods, over the mountains, or even across the lake, with only what you'll need to survive for two nights and three days. You'll rest on breezy overlooks, discover secret, hidden swimming spots, cook over a campfire, and sleep out under the stars, listening to owls hooting. Your counselors have been doing this for years and will look forward to teaching you the ways of the wilderness.

You are in for a wonderful time! So, pack your enthusiasm and your sense of humor along with your socks, and come to Camp Wolf Trail. We are ready for the fun to begin, and we know that you are too.

See you soon!

All of us here at Camp Wolf Trail

# Packing List

Due to our simple camp lifestyle, and our even-more-rustic wilderness trips, anything you bring may get wet, dirty, lost, or all three combined. So, leave the special stuff at home.

## Do bring:

### Daily camp supplies

☐ Shorts and T-shirts for warm weather

☐ Clothes for cooler temperatures (Fleece clothing is good for camping because it dries quickly.)

☐ Socks (Wool is good for hiking because it also dries quickly.)

☐ Hiking shoes or boots for trips, and everyday shoes for camp (Be sure to break in new boots or shoes before you get here!)

☐ Old sneakers/water shoes for canoeing and creek hikes

☐ Swimming gear: suit, sunscreen, towel

☐ Sheets, blanket, and pillow for your bunk in camp

☐ Bathroom items: towel, toothbrush, toothpaste, shampoo, soap (although we've noticed that some campers' soaps don't get used too often!)

### Wilderness trip supplies

The basics: a comfortable backpack, lightweight sleeping bag, roll-up camping pad, mess kit (plate, cup, fork, and spoon) water bottle, flashlight with extra batteries, water-proof poncho

Optional: camping knife (check it in with your counselor when you arrive), camping pillow, compass, hat, bandanna

If you wear glasses, bring a cord to hold them safely around your neck, so you don't lose them when boating or rock climbing.

## Other optional items

☐ Good books

☐ Portable games such as cards and cribbage, crossword puzzles

☐ Paper, stamps, envelopes, pen, addresses (Your parents and friends will want to hear from you!)

☐ Art supplies, journal, nature guides, binoculars, musical instrument (if it's not too fragile), or other hobby supplies

☐ Pocket money (no more than $20, though)

Please **do not bring** any electronics or a cell phone. They don't survive getting wet, dirty, or lost. And besides, who needs them? You'll be hiking in the woods and swimming in the lake most of the time. Who would you text? A squirrel? A fish? Enjoy being free of screens (except the kind that keeps bugs out) for two weeks!

# ZEE'S STORY
# BOYS
# CAMP

*Three fingers crammed into a sharp crevice, toes shoved into a narrow toehold, a gusty wind at his back, and a vertical drop ending in ice-cold water yawning below him. "How'd I get myself in this fix?" Zee wondered, dangling on the rock face, sweat stinging his eyes. "Oh, yeah, that's right. I asked for it. Ah well. Nowhere to go but up, I guess."*

*Zee stretched his free hand up above his head as far as it could go, feeling blindly for a bump, a crack, a notch—anything to grab. Yes! His raw fingertips found a one-inch niche. It wasn't much, but it was enough. Carefully, Zee slid his fingers into the niche. His free foot—the left one—found a knotty root, and Zee shifted his weight onto it, knowing that roots were risky. It was never a good move to trust a root. But this one held—just long enough for Zee to lift his body, plant his right hand on the top of the rock, and then heave first his leg, then his upper* body, to safety. For a second, Zee lay motionless, except for panting. Then he scrambled to his feet. He raised both arms above his head and howled like a wolf.

*Aroo-oo!*

*From below came a chorus of answering howls. Aroo-oo! Then chanting. "Zee! Zee! Zee!"*

*Zee grinned. He strode to the edge of the rock, rose up on his toes, and dove. Down, down, down he shot and then swoosh, slid with a clean slice into the deep, frigid water of O'Mannitt's Cove.*

And that, *he thought,* is how it's done.

*The boys were still chanting his name when Zee bobbed to the surface, breathless from the shocking cold and from the exhilaration of his dive. When they saw his head emerge, the rest of the boys stampeded into the water, hooting and howling as they splashed and crashed toward Zee to congratulate him. Their counselor, Carlos, paddled over in his kayak.*

*"So," said Carlos, "you've just aced a Camp Wolf Trail tradition: the Dead Man's Dive off Big Boulder. Congratulations."*

*"Thanks," said Zee.*

*"Was it as great as you thought it would be?"* asked Zee's best camp buddy, Will.

*"No,"* said Zee. *"It was better."* He splashed Will. *"So, go on. Now it's your turn."*

*Carlos laughed. "That's right,"* he said. *"Go for it."*

*Zee laughed, too. He and Will had asked for permission to do the Dead Man's Dive a thousand times last summer. Doing the dive was a privilege that had to be earned. A counselor had to agree to teach you how to do it. Who'd have thought that the way he and Will would finally get the go-ahead would involve an octopus, pies, and toilet paper?*

*It all started on this summer's first day of camp. . .*

# Chapter One

"*YA-HOO!*" Zee Doyle threw his head back and hollered as loud as he could. This was it, the moment he'd been looking forward to—crazy impatient—for months. Finally, he was back at Camp Wolf Trail, his favorite place on Earth. Zee waved good-bye to his mom and dad as they drove off, and then he spun around and took a deep breath. Yup, there it was, the classic Wolf Trail smell: sun on pine needles, bug spray, and a whiff of lake-sharp air. Zee let loose the epic howl that had been building in his chest since he left camp last summer: *Aroo-oo!* He listened for a return howl—that's how he and his best friend at camp, Will, located each other—but there was none, so Zee figured Will probably hadn't arrived yet.

*Slam!* A screen door flew open, hitting the outside of the camp office, making a bush full of brown birds take off twittering.

"Zee!" It was Max, one of Zee's favorite camp counselors from last year. Max tossed his clipboard onto the grass and lifted Zee up into a bear hug. Max was tall, so his hugs were polar bear hugs. "Welcome back!"

"Thanks!" said Zee. "Is Will here yet?"

Max shrugged his wide shoulders. "I haven't seen him, but he might have checked in with some-body else." Max tilted his head toward Zee's trunk. "Put your trunk on the golf cart and I'll drive it up to your cabin later," he said. "You're in Birch. Carlos is your cabin counselor again, like he was in Cedar last year."

"Great," said Zee. Carlos was another favor-ite counselor of Zee's.

"No point in sending an old-timer like you on a map quest to your cabin like the newbies," said Max. "You know all the trails better than I do."

"Almost all," said Zee. He grinned at Max with eager curiosity. "I don't know the secret trail to Hidden Falls. How about a hint?"

"Nope," said Max, shaking his head slowly. "No way. Like everybody else who's ever been, I promised never to tell how to get there. You'll have to find Hidden Falls by yourself."

"I will," said Zee. "Well, not by myself. Will and I are going to find Hidden Falls together this summer, for sure. And by the way, we're *also* finally going to get to do the Dead Man's Dive off Big Boulder, too."

"I bet you will," said Max. "Busy summer for you two. Good luck. Meanwhile, get going. Carlos and the guys in Birch are waiting for you."

"Okay!" said Zee. He heaved his trunk onto to the golf cart, flung his backpack over his shoulder, and set off for Birch at a run, eager to find Will and get the fun started. Will had been a newbie last summer. He'd been quiet and standoffish at first, but Carlos had encouraged Zee to befriend him. So, in the good old Camp Wolf Trail tradition, Zee did. Both boys had soon discovered that they liked to pull practical jokes, and after that they became an inseparable team for the rest of the summer.

This was Zee's third summer at camp. Max was right: by now, Zee knew the trails as well as his own backyard. He took the shortcut to Birch, making a quick left onto an old trail that was really just a deer path. The tall grass swished his legs as he jogged steadily, slowing only to duck beneath a gigantic bough that made a leafy arch above the trail. On the other side, he quickened his pace when he spotted a small, weedy clearing up ahead. There was Birch Cabin, looking sleepy in the dappled light. A carpet of furry moss stretched down the shady side of the roof and tangled ivy crept up the outside corners.

"Yo, Birch!" Zee shouted. "Anybody home?"

"Yo!" came answering shouts. The cabin door burst open and a stampede of boys blasted out yelling, "Zee!" Most of the boys leapt, their feet never even touching the two steps that led from the door to the grass below. Zee saw Carlos and some new guys, but no Will.

"Zee-Man!" said Carlos. "We've been waiting for you, buddy!"

"I'll help with your bag," said Yasu. He took the pack from Zee's shoulder and led the way up the steps into the cabin.

"Come on in," said Carlos, holding open the door with one hand. "I'm really glad you're in Birch, Zee."

"Me, too," said Zee.

Yasu punched Zee's arm and joked, "Guess they decided to put all the cool kids in one cabin. Remember Jim and Erik from last summer? They're going to be in Birch, too, but they're not here yet."

"We saved you a bed," said Nate. He smacked the mattress on the lower bunk, raising a mushroom-cloud of dust that filled the space up to the bottom of the upper bunk.

"Thanks," coughed Zee, laughing.

"Zee, meet Vik and Sean and Kareem," said Carlos. "They're newbies. We'll have another new guy, too, named Zack, but he hasn't arrived. Guys, this is Zee."

"Hey," the boys said to one another.

"Zee is one half of the dynamic duo, Will-n-Zee," added Yasu.

"Where *is* Will?" asked Nate.

"I was going to ask you the same thing," said Zee. "Where is he?"

Carlos shrugged, saying, "He must not be at camp yet."

"Zee, check it out! You got a postcard already," said Yasu, handing a card to Zee.

"Say what? A postcard?" asked Zee. "Who from?" Zee took the postcard from Yasu. On one side, there was a picture of a wolf. Zee flipped it over. On the other side, the card was addressed to him, in care of Camp Wolf Trail. The hand-written message read:

Zee, Due to an unfortunate change of
plans, I won't be coming to camp this
summer. Sorry. Your friend, Will

Zee felt socked in the stomach.

"What's it say?" asked Nate. He looked over Zee's shoulder, trying to read the card.

"Will's not coming," said Zee, not believing it himself. He skimmed the words again, hoping he'd misunderstood. But how could he have misread two sentences—one of them only one word long?

"Aw, man," said Yasu. "No Will? That stinks. You and Will were the two funniest guys at camp last summer. How will we have any laughs if Will's not here?"

"Let me see that card," said Nate.

Zee handed Nate the card, thinking: *Without Will, I'm Zee-for-zero. I can't pull off jokes or tricks without him! He's my swim buddy, my cabin mate, my best camp friend, my partner in pranks. Without Will, pfft—there go all the plans we've been emailing back and forth all winter. What a rotten start to the summer.*

Carlos put his hand on Zee's shoulder. "Sorry Will can't make it, man."

Nate gave Zee the card back. "At least he sent you a cool photo of a wolf," he said.

*Yeah, that's appropriate because now I'm a* lone *wolf,* thought Zee. He flopped onto the bottom bunk. The mattress felt scratchy and uncomfortable. *Camp's gonna be lousy without Will. Even this bunk feels awful.*

"Ow!" Zee sat up fast. Something sharp had poked him through the mattress. Zee felt around on the mattress, trying to find it so that he could punch it down. That's when he heard the muffled laughter coming from below him. "What's going on?" he said.

"GOTCHA!" howled someone. It was Will! He slid out from beneath the bed, raised his fists above his head like a winning prizefighter, and hooted triumphantly, "Nailed! You really thought I wasn't coming, didn't you? Oh, man! I really fooled you this time."

"Will, you skunk!" Zee laughed happily. He gave Will a friendly shove that made him totter backward.

"Well done, Will," Nate said. "I've got to hand it to you. You tricked the trickster. You pulled a Will-n-Zee on Zee."

"I've been hiding under that bed choking on dust for hours," Will said, swatting the dust off his shorts. "But it was worth it. No question. I fooled *all* of you—even you, Carlos. You guys should've heard yourselves!" Will put on a low voice as he imitated Carlos. "Carlos was like, 'Sorry.'" Then

Will put on a squeaky voice to imitate Yasu. "And Yasu was like, 'Aw, *man*!'"

Will laughed so hard he had to clutch his stomach. The new boys joined in, and so did Yasu, Nate, Zee, and Carlos.

Nate held his fist to his mouth and pretended to be a sportscaster. "Watch out, sports fans!" he intoned. "Will-n-Zee, the practical jokesters, are back in business. Looks like it'll be another summer full of thrills, chills, tricks, and spills. You never know *what's* gonna happen with Will-n-Zee around."

"He's not kidding about the kidding," Yasu explained to Vik, Sean, and Kareem. "Last summer, when we were in Cedar Cabin together, Will-n-Zee pulled a good one. The rest of us came back from archery or something—we hadn't been gone long—and we couldn't get inside the cabin because they'd stuffed it full of balled-up newspapers."

"How about the time they freaked us out by cleaning up the cabin?" said Nate. "We woke up and the floor was scrubbed, the towels were folded, the trunks were all packed and ship-shape. The cabin was totally clean. Carlos was like, 'What happened here? Am I in an alternate universe?'"

"Yeah," added Yasu. "Cedar Cabin even *smelled* good, not like sweaty socks like it usually did."

"Like Birch already does!" said Sean.

"That prank was funny and it was, you know, *nice*, too," said Carlos. He shook his head and grinned at Zee and Will. "I still don't know how you did it so quietly."

"We're not telling," said Will. He poked Zee. "Secret unto death. Right, partner?"

"Right," said Zee. "But stay tuned, campers. We've been emailing ideas back and forth all winter, and we've got some lulus and doozies planned for this summer." Zee loved to make up new words, so now he said, "Word of the day, guys: lulu-doozies."

All the boys groaned and cheered and tossed stuff—socks, pillows, tennis balls, rolled up towels, and flip-flops—at Zee and Will.

Zee ducked a flying pillow. And then, because it was the only way to express how happy and relieved he was to be reunited with Will, he howled with glee: "*Lulu-doozie!*"

And Will answered with a long, loud howl of his own: "*Lulu-doozie, aroo-oo!*"

# Chapter Two

"So, the good news is, I'm here, with about a million great ideas for practical jokes," said Will. He twirled a basketball on the tip of his finger as he and Zee sat on the steps of Birch. "But, the bad news is, I'm in Pawpaw Cabin, not Birch."

"Are we at least in the same cluster?" asked Zee. Clusters were groups of campers who teamed up on theme days and did outings and chores together.

"Yes," said Will. "We're both Isabels."

"Isa whats?" asked Zee.

"Isabels," said Will. "This summer, clusters are named after the punch lines of knock-knock jokes. So we're Isabels, short for 'Isabel Necessary on a Bike?'"

"I like it," chuckled Zee. "Typical Camp Wolf Trail. And I'm glad we're in the same cluster. That'll make it easier for us to make plans. Speaking of. . ." He lowered his voice and glanced back over his shoulder to be sure no one would hear him. "Let's meet at the tennis courts later to talk about getting rid of the you-know-what. Okay?"

"Sure," said Will. "I'll head over to Pawpaw now, but meet you in about an hour." He tucked the basketball under his arm and smiled. "Just like Nate said—Will-n-Zee are back in business."

"Finally!" said Zee. "I've been waiting all year."

Will left, and Zee went back inside Birch. Pretty soon Jim and the new guy Zack arrived, and in no time, Zee was running a cookie throwdown to decide whose cookies were best: Zack's chocolate chips or Kareem's peanut butter bars. Both cookies were so good that Erik, another old camper, declared it a tie, but only after everybody had stuffed himself. Zee stuck with his cabin mates when they all went to the lake to take their swim tests. But when the guys went to O'Mannitt's Cove for a splash fight, Zee slipped away to meet Will.

The two tricksters had a lot to talk about. Just before the end of camp last summer, Zee had been on the receiving end of a long-running Camp Wolf Trail practical joke. The Hot Potato Octopus had been planted in Zee's stuff. The octopus was a hideous, screaming yellow, extra-large stuffed animal complete with button suction cups running down eight dangly arms, bald spots where its plush had been worn away, and thin spots where its stuffing had fallen out over the years. It smelled ripe, too. The tradition was that anyone caught with the Hot Potato Octopus got a pie in the face tossed by the person who'd planted the octopus on him. Luckily, no one had been around when Zee found the octopus stuffed in his sleeping bag last summer. He had hidden it and told only Will.

Now, when Will got to the courts, Zee said, "I'm still kind of bummed about getting stuck with the stupid octopus." Zee made up a new word to express how he felt. "Somebody picked me to be *octo-pied*."

"Shake it off," said Will. "I can see how you might not want to get creamed with a pie, but look at it this way: being one of the few people to get octo-pied at Camp Wolf Trail is a badge of honor."

Zee grinned in spite of himself. "Some honor."

"No, it *is*," Will went on, "especially for you. I think you were chosen deliberately. In your case, the octopus was dumped on you because you're so good at practical jokes. It's as if the Hot Potato Octopus dumpster was saying, 'You can dish it out, Zee. Now, let's see if you can take it.' I bet the dumpster meant it as a challenge. Everybody

knows you're tricky and you're smart. Plus, you have a brilliant partner-in-crime—me. The dumpster knew we'd flip the octopus thing around, put our own spin on it." He slid Zee a sly smile. "And that's exactly what we did, right?"

"Right," agreed Zee. He smiled, too. Since camp was almost over when the octopus was dumped on him, Zee and Will had hit upon a brilliant idea: Zee sneaked the octopus home in his luggage. "I bet no one's ever done that before. It probably drove whoever dumped the octopus on me crazy. He had to stew all year wondering what the heck was going on. Plus, it gave us a whole year to come up with a plan to plant it on somebody else."

"Tonight's the night," said Will, as he shot the basketball at the rickety, net-less, rusted ring that served as a basketball hoop at Camp Wolf Trail. "The time has come to put our plan into action."

"Planning has been cool," said Zee. All winter, in their emails, for secrecy and just for fun, the boys called the octopus the "supotco," which was "octopus" backwards. "But I'll be glad to get rid of the supotco. I sure hope I don't get caught trying to get rid of it."

"Hey, if you get caught, I will, too," said Will, shooting another basket. He was so much taller than he'd been last summer that he sank the shot with ease. "I hope Skeeter-the-cook won't mind making two pies." Will passed the basketball to Zee. "I won't let you get pied-in-the-face alone."

"Thanks!" said Zee, catching the pass, extra glad that Will was his friend.

Shooting hoops made the boys thirsty, so they stopped off at the hose next to the dining hall to get a drink of water before they went back to their cabins.

"See you at dinner," said Will. "Be sure Carlos brings his guitar so he'll have to stay at the campfire till the end."

"He always does," said Zee. First-night-of-camp dinner was always a cookout down at the lake, and Carlos always played his guitar so the old campers could teach the new guys the camp songs. "It's tradition."

"Yeah," said Will, "just like the octopus is a tradition. But *it's* a tradition you and I have changed a little bit."

"We've Will-n-Zeed it," said Zee, "and—" Zee stopped short. He elbowed Will hard because just then, Skeeter Malone, the camp cook, came out of the dining hall, wiping his hands on his apron. Skeeter's dog, Cookie, followed him. When Cookie saw the boys, he leapt up on them, greeting them with slurpy, doggish enthusiasm.

"Hi, there, boys," said Skeeter. "Welcome back."

"Thanks," said Zee and Will in unison, trying to sound casual.

Skeeter took a deep breath. "Nice breeze," he said. "Smells good. And you know, a breeze like this carries sound—and conversations—really well."

Zee froze. Will looked at him in horror. Clearly, Skeeter had overheard their conversation about the octopus. Would he give them away?

But Skeeter winked. "I was wondering when that old octopus would turn up," he said. "It disappeared at the end of camp last summer. That's never happened before. You two *have* changed the tradition." He smiled at the boys. "Don't worry. I won't spill the beans. I'll be too busy. Seems like I've got some baking to do." He looked down at Cookie and patted his head. "You love a good pie, don't you, Cookie?"

Cookie wagged his tail so hard it banged against Skeeter's leg.

"*Everybody* loves pie," said Will. "No question."

"Hey," said Zee. "You just gave me a great idea!" He turned to Skeeter and asked, "Would you like to help us change the tradition a little more?"

Before Skeeter answered, Will jabbed Zee hard. "Don't let him in on our plan," he muttered, frowning.

"Why not?" asked Zee. He was a little surprised. He and Will usually saw eye-to-eye. "Trust me, you'll be glad." Zee turned to Skeeter and asked, "What do you say?"

★ ★ ★

Zee usually ate about twenty hot dogs at the first-night-of-camp cookout by the lake. But tonight, he was too nervous to eat much. Nobody noticed. Everybody was too busy eating, singing along with Carlos, laughing, clapping, cheering, and shouting out the names of their favorite camp songs for Carlos to play next. Nobody noticed when Will and Zee slipped away from the campfire, either, because they were singing at the top of their lungs:

*This land is your land, this land is my land, from California, to the New York island . . .*

And then Carlos led the old campers in the jokey camp version:

*Wolf Trail is your camp, Wolf Trail is my camp, from the wrecky rec hall, to the splintery boat ramp . . .*

The sun had just dipped behind the trees as Zee and Will left the fire circle. It was a clear night, perfect for an undercover mission. The crickets chirped and the fireflies flashed in agreement. Without speaking, Zee and Will headed up the path that led back through the trees. They stopped before entering the clearing around Birch, peering ahead to see if anyone was in the cabin.

"The coast is clear," said Will.

"Game on," said Zee.

The boys sprinted to the cabin and up the steps. Zee's eyes refocused to the dark inside. It was strange to find Birch empty. The room had a dank smell, sort of like stagnant swamp water.

Zee flipped on the battery-powered lantern. With one last check out the door to make sure no was coming, Zee slid a lump wrapped in a blanket out from under his bunk. He unwrapped it carefully, as if it might come alive and reach out and grab him.

"Boo!" said Will.

Zee yelped, "Whoa!" Startled, he stepped back, dropping the octopus. Eight bright yellow tentacles flopped out onto the floor in a jumbled pile.

"Yikes," said Will, shading his eyes. "It's brighter than I remembered."

"I washed it," laughed Zee. "I glued reflective strips on it, too."

"It's cool how it glows in the dark when the light hits it," said Will. "You better hide it under your shirt."

Zee stuffed the yellow octopus under his T-shirt. It was sort of scratchy. He was just about to click off the lantern when Will grabbed his arm.

"Wait a second," he said. "I think we've got a golden opportunity here to pull a Will-n-Zee."

"What do you have in mind?" asked Zee with a flash of reluctance. He didn't want to risk blowing the octopus plan.

Will grinned wickedly. "Redecoration."

"Okay," said Zee. "But let's redecorate *your* cabin—Pawpaw. It makes me nervous to stay here in Birch one second longer."

"It's okay with me to put our paws on Pawpaw," said Will. "Let's go."

The boys sprinted over to Pawpaw, set to work, and in record time, the inside of Pawpaw Cabin was unrecognizable. Zee held the cabin door open for Will, who closed it silently behind himself. Zee's heart was beating fast, even though everything was going according to plan. Will led the way back into the woods, where a chorus of crickets sounded like a million people talking at once. When the boys emerged from the woods near the lake, Cookie was waiting for them.

"Want to join in the fun, Cookie?" asked Will.

Cookie wagged his tail and followed the boys to the cove. A full moon hung in the sky, its reflection shining on the still lake, lighting a wide path across it.

"There it is," said Zee, nodding toward Carlos's bright red-and-yellow kayak, which stood out in the moonlight. Carlos had left it propped upside down near the little boat ramp, its black paddle secured underneath. Carlos was obsessed with kayaks. Every summer he brought his own kayak to camp. The boys teased him that he was half-man, half-kayak because he was so often sitting in his kayak, paddling across the lake, that they hardly ever saw his legs.

"I've got to ask Carlos to teach me how to kayak this summer," said Zee. He moved the stuffed animal to one arm and flipped the kayak over. It made a hollow *thunk* as it settled, rocking on the ground until it was still. The paddle fell to the side. "Where should I put the octopus?"

"Here, let me," said Will. He plucked the octopus out of Zee's arms. Cookie followed him as Will placed the octopus in the cockpit of the kayak. Will pointed its silly smiling face toward the main trail. Then he wrapped two of the octopus's arms around the paddle and tilted it so that it looked like the octopus was using it.

"Perfect," said Zee. Will was such a great partner-in-pranks!

"Carlos is going to freak," said Will.

"Yeah," said Zee. "But you do think he's the right guy to octo-pie, don't you? I don't want to hurt anybody's feelings. A newbie wouldn't understand, and even an old camper might get bent out of shape. Carlos will be cool with it, right? He won't get mad."

"No way!" said Will. "He'll *appreciate* being Will-n-Zeed. No question. He'll get a kick out of being our first victim of the summer."

"Actually, he'll get a pie out of it," said Zee.

The boys laughed quietly and high-fived. Zee wished he could take a picture of the two of them and the octopus sitting in the kayak. Instead, he saluted. "Bye, supotco," he said. "Nice knowing ya."

*Swoosh! Woosh!* The boys gasped at the sound, stepping away from the kayak into the protection of the trees by the lake.

Cookie looked up and his eyebrows lifted into little triangles as if to say, "Who goes there?"

"Don't you start howling and give away our secret, Dog," whispered Zee.

Cookie seemed to understand. He sniffed the air a few times and then seemed to forget about the rustling in the woods.

The boys relaxed. If Cookie hadn't sensed a person, then the sound must have been nothing but the breeze off the lake blowing through the pine branches, or a big bird like an owl just swooping by to check them out.

Cookie ambled to the water's edge. He waded in belly-deep, looking at the boys as though inviting them to join him.

"Sorry, Cookie, you know the rules. No swimming without a lifeguard, not even for a dog," said Will. "Come on out now."

Agreeably, Cookie bounded out of the water. He ran up to the boys and shook his fur out, spraying them with lake water and damp dog hair.

"Great idea to invite Cookie along," joked Zee, wiping his face. "Now we reek of wet dog."

"I've smelled worse," said Will. "So have you. Come on. Let's get back to the campfire before somebody realizes that we're missing."

# Chapter Three

Slipping silently through the shadows, Zee and Will returned to the campfire. They hung back, sitting behind Yasu, so that no one would ask why they were out of breath, why they smelled like wet dog, or why the wet dog in question had suddenly appeared. Good old Cookie stuck by them in the darkness. Max and another counselor, Simon, had built a campfire that roared inside the stone fire ring. They had piled the logs into a structure that lifted the flames up three feet high. The fire crackled and sizzled, sending sparks high into the night sky.

"*Great green globs of greasy grimey gopher guts,*" the campers sang, going for the record as World's

Worst and Loudest Singers as they hit the ending, "*And I forgot my spoo—oo—oon . . .*"

The boys cheered for themselves, and Max said, "Okay, guys, congratulations. That was totally terrible."

The boys cheered again, and Max had to hold up his hands for quiet before he could go on. "Okay!" he said. "Games and activities, crafts and chores, and outings all begin tomorrow, which means it's time for bed. Simon and I are on fire duty. We'll be heading down to the lake to get water. Carlos will lead you on your way back to the cabins."

"No!" everyone groaned. "Not yet!"

"The moon's full," Zee said to Will loud enough for the kids near them to hear.

"Oh, yeah?" said Will. "I can't see it through all the trees."

"Then let's go down to the lake with Max and Simon," said Zee, "so we can see the moon over the water without the trees blocking it."

"Good idea," said Will. He poked Yasu in the back and asked, "Want to come?"

"Sure," said Yasu. He sounded surprised and pleased that Will and Zee were including him. Then, just as Will and Zee had thought he would, Yasu yelled, "Hey, everybody! We're going back to the cabins by way of the lake. Gotta see the full moon on the water. Come on, Carlos, sing us on our way. Everybody, follow me."

Will and Zee exchanged silent looks of triumph. Yasu *always* liked to lead.

All the campers stood, stretched, and then some of the boys headed to their cabins and others—mostly from Pawpaw and Birch—followed Yasu toward the lake. Max and Simon swung water buckets, chatting with Tyler, one of the guys from Pawpaw. Carlos looped his guitar strap over his shoulder and sang as he walked:

*Oh, Mister Moon, Moon, Mister Silver Moon, won't you please shine down on me?*

*Oh Mister Moon, Moon, Mister Silver Moon, hiding behind that tree.*

*All these guys are telling you, to Camp Wolf Trail they'll be true.*

*So Mister Moon, Moon, Mister Silver Moon,
won't you please shine down on,*

*Please shine down on, please shine down on me?*

Zee and Will joined the song and the group of boys. They acted casual and unhurried as they strolled along, as though they had not a care in the world.

Ahead, Zee saw the guys in Birch. Seemed like a good group this year. Behind Yasu there was Jim, whose head stuck up because he was so much taller than everyone else, walking with Erik and Zack. Nate was talking to Vik and Sean and flashing his flashlight up into the trees as if he were looking for something. Kareem, another Birch newbie, danced around trying to keep a daddy-long-legs on his arm.

The way the boys jostled one another, and the way they were the same but different, reminded Zee of wolves and how they stuck to their packs for just about everything—living together, eating together, and traveling together. He thought—not for the first time—how appropriately named Camp Wolf Trail was.

The lake came into view, looking magical with a wide swath of moonlight gleaming on it. Zee called, "Hey, Carlos! Will you, Max, and Simon life guard us if we go for a moonlight swim?"

"Okay," said Carlos. "If you've taken your swim test, turn your pegs, get your buddy, and swim."

"Word of the day, Campers!" shouted Zee. "We're *moon-a-luna-dips*. Get it?"

Everyone groaned, and Jim said, "I still haven't changed out of my swim trunks since this afternoon's swim. And I still haven't dried out. So I'm ready for a moon-a-luna-dip."

"That's the beauty of living in your bathing suit," said Nate. "You're already ready to swim."

"I'm already ready, too," said Yasu.

"Already ready, three," joked Vik.

"Yeah," said Tyler. "I'm already ready four for the swim. No need for sunscreen, either."

"That means it's time for a plunge! Who's in?" shouted Erik. The rest of the boys cheered and picked up the pace, zooming down the path to the lake. Zee and Will kept up with their friends, trying to blend in. Zee was glad they couldn't hear his heart pounding.

Yasu was first in the pack, as usual. At the dock, he came to a sudden stop. "Whoa," he said quietly. He pointed to Carlos's kayak. "What is *that*?"

Zee and Will were delighted. With moonlight shining like a spotlight and bouncing off the water, the octopus in the kayak looked even weirder than they remembered.

Now all the boys were talking at once. "Carlos, what's in your . . . ?"

"What in the . . . ?"

"Who?"

Carlos walked slowly up to the kayak. He plucked the octopus out of his boat and spun around to face the boys. The tentacles spun, too.

No one said a thing. Zee couldn't tell if Carlos was mad or not. He sure hoped he wasn't.

Carlos lifted the octopus above his head and said, "Nailed."

Now all the boys exploded into cheers. Their noisy laughter shook the woods with more crazy cackles than a camp full of monkeys.

"I just made up a song!" said Max. He sang to Carlos:

*When the moon hits your eye like a big Skeeter pie, you've been Oc-toed.*

"Hot potato!" shouted Carlos. He burst out laughing and threw the octopus to Yasu, who caught it and then tossed it in the air. The boys passed it around like it really *was* a hot potato that would burn their fingers if they touched it. Finally, Carlos snagged it and kept it.

"Okay, all right," he said cheerfully. "I might as well take my medicine and get it over with. Forget swimming. Somebody better run ahead and tell Skeeter to ring the cowbell so everybody'll come to the dining hall. Looks like I'm having pie-in-the-face for a bedtime snack." He shook his head.

"I gotta hand it to whoever did this to me. Well done, octo-dumpster."

"You know what?" said Jim as they all headed up to the dining hall. "This looks like a Will-n-Zee to me." He turned to the jokesters. "Did you two geniuses do this?"

Will and Zee shrugged. "You'll soon see," said Zee. "The dumpster gets to throw the pie, right?"

Just then, the camp cowbell jangled loud and clear. As the boys from the lake reached the picnic table outside the dining hall, other campers emerged out of the woods and their cabins, squinting, yawning, and trying to figure out what was

going on. They knew the sound of the bell meant "Come now, or miss something good."

Skeeter scanned the crowd. "Carlos, my friend," he said, "come take a seat."

"It's my sincere pleasure," said Carlos. He took off his guitar and carefully put it far away from the picnic table. Then he bowed to the campers, grinned, and sat down near Skeeter. A chocolate pie, covered with whipped cream and decorated with a single red cherry, sat on the table, illuminated by lantern light. "Pardon me, where's my napkin?" asked Carlos.

"Where's your bib?" someone shouted.

"Where's the hose?" added someone else.

"It is a time-honored tradition that the guy who plants the octopus gets to toss the pie at the one he plants it upon," said Skeeter. "This time, the dumpsters were Camp Wolf Trail's favorite wise guys, Will and Zee." All the campers cheered as Skeeter ceremoniously handed the pie to Zee, saying, "Zee gets to do the honors because he's the one who had the octopus last."

"On the count of three," said Skeeter, speaking to Zee. "Then Octo-Pie!"

Zee and Will gave each other a smile in cahoots. The crowd of campers gathered around, laughing and cheering and hollering. Zee could have sworn he even heard someone yodeling.

"One."

"Two."

"Three!"

Zee lifted the pie as if to throw it and then . . .

He put it down. He placed it on the table carefully and stepped away from it.

"Hey!" hollered the campers. "What're you doing? What's the deal?"

Zee held up his hands for quiet. "Will and I want to change the Hot Potato Octopus tradition," said Zee, "and Skeeter agreed to help us. So, instead of Carlos getting a pie in the face, Skeeter made PIE FOR EVERYBODY!"

The boys cheered louder than ever. Skeeter flung open the door to the dining hall and the wild pie eaters thundered in. The long tables were dotted with pies of all sorts. "Grab a fork and dive in!" said Skeeter. And nobody waited to be told twice.

Carlos thumped Will and Zee on the back. "I owe you one, guys."

"That's what we were hoping you'd say," said Zee. "We have a favor to ask you. How about telling us how to find Hidden Falls?"

"Sorry," said Carlos. "That I cannot do."

"We thought you might say that, too," said Will. "So we have a backup favor. How about teaching us how to do Dead Man's Dive off Big Boulder into O'Mannitt's Cove?"

"You're on," said Carlos. "It's a deal."

"Thanks!" said Will and Zee together.

Then they got to work sharing one of Skeeter's pies—apple with raisins in it—and eating it quickly.

"Look at you two," said Tyler. "Camp Wolf Trail's funnymen are giving new meaning to the phrase *wolf it down*. What's your hurry?"

"Let's just say the night's not over yet," said Will mischievously, "and neither are the surprises."

Tyler smacked his forehead, shaking his head in pretend despair. "I can't take any more," he said. "You guys are wearing us out with all this fun—and it's just our first day."

Will and Zee practically wore themselves out laughing as they stood outside and heard the Pawpaw Cabin campers' howls of delight and surprise upon discovering that the inside of their cabin was festooned with toilet paper. Swoops and loops of paper hung from the beams, wound up the bunk posts, and mummified the boys' trunks. A dense spider's web of white filled the interior of the cabin so that the boys had to bat their way through to their beds.

"Yeah, it's funny," said Simon, the Pawpaw counselor. "But guess what, folks? You've gotta re-roll all that toilet paper. That's our allotment for the summer. You don't want to waste it."

"Aw, man!" the boys groaned.

Zee chuckled. "Word of the day, Pawpaw Cabiners: *Roller-rama-drama*!" Zee turned to Will and said, "This is when I leave for Birch. You better help your buddies."

"Okay," said Will. "Roller-rama-drama, man."

"Listen, thanks, Will," said Zee. "I gotta say, this has to have been the greatest first night of Camp Wolf Trail ever. All our plans were good, and everything went perfectly. We didn't find out how to get to Hidden Falls, but we're going to do Dead Man's Dive."

"Yeah," said Will. "And we'll find the Falls. No question." He turned to go inside Pawpaw, and then in an unusually serious tone he said, "One thing, though. Don't forget what I said before. No bringing anybody else in on our plans, especially without asking me. Finding the Falls, whatever we do. It's you and me, Will-n-Zee, right?"

"Uh, yeah, sure, you and me," said Zee, a little taken aback. "Right."

"Okay then," said Will. "See you tomorrow."

Will loped up the steps to Pawpaw with the long-legged strides his new height gave him. Zee watched him go, feeling puzzled and just a bit like he'd been scolded. He shook it off. Will was right, of course. Will-n-Zee needed nobody else. As Will would say, no question.

# Chapter Four

Carlos was true to his word. The very next afternoon, he began instructing Zee and Will to prepare for their climb and dive. Carlos led Zee and Will to Big Boulder at O'Mannitt's Cove and painstakingly taught them how to scale the giant rock face. Then they watched as he dove off Big Boulder into the water. Carlos insisted that Zee and Will needed a couple days of instruction so that they'd be really ready to climb and dive safely. They squeezed the lessons in just after Arts and Crafts while the rest of Birch was at Archery. Zee was a little sorry to miss Archery with the rest of the Birch Cabin guys; they were having a really funny mock Robin

Hood Archery Contest, and the prize was going to be a sack of chocolate gold coins. But hey! He'd wanted to do Dead Man's Dive for three years, so he was psyched to have his chance at last.

When Carlos thought Will and Zee were ready, he finally gave them permission to do their climb and dive. It felt great—that moment of triumph in front of the Birch and Pawpaw guys. After they both dove, all the guys walked back to the beach and dock where they usually swam. They had to step aside to let a small pickup truck come through. Attached to the truck like a rattling caboose was a trailer carrying a dozen colorful kayaks.

"Aw, Carlos, you shouldn't have," joked Will. "Kayaks as gifts for us all? That was really nice of you."

Carlos laughed. "I wish I could have bought kayaks for you all," he said. "But these are just on loan. Birch Cabin's going on a kayak trip to camp out on Spikey Island for a night."

"Just Birch?" asked Will. "Not Pawpaw? Not the Isabels?"

"Birch first," said Carlos, "but your turn will come, Will, don't worry."

Zee could see that Will was disappointed, so he decided to distract him by pulling some stunts to make him laugh. "Hey, guys," Zee said to the boys. "You know what we need to refresh ourselves after our swim in O'Mannitt's Cove? A swim."

"You got it," said the boys. They headed for the pegboard, jostling for a turn to flip their tags from green to red. Then they ran to the end of the dock and waited next to their swim buddies, their toes wrapped around the long edge of the wooden platform. After the last of the boys had flipped his peg, Carlos grabbed the foam rescue tube, then walked out to the edge of the water and blew his whistle, the boys' signal that it was okay to jump in.

"Word of the day, guys," said Zee. "Plungiferous!"

With Tarzan whoops, piercing shrieks of joy, wolf howls, and shouts of *Plungiferous!* the boys threw themselves into the water. Zee hung back on the dock, waiting for his friends to come back up to surface.

"It's your lucky day, Campers," he said. "I'm going to show you the perfect dive. Perfect! You want to see what years of swim team and diving lessons gets you? Watch this!" Zee bent his knees with exaggerated precision, made a perfect arrow with his hands above his head, and pushed off with the dock in slow motion, arcing in a smooth dive. Then, midway into the water, he flapped his arms and kicked wildly, clownishly contorting himself. "Whoa-oh! Whoa! Aaaaaack!" Zee hit the surface with an enormous smack, sending water splashing everywhere.

"Nice job, Zee!" The boys laughed and shouted and splashed water at Zee when his head came back up above the water.

"Good thing you didn't goof around like that when you jumped off Big Boulder," said Jim. "We'd have called it Dud Man's Dive."

"No, really?" asked Zee, pretending incomprehension. "That wasn't good? Okay. Let me try again. Watch *this*."

"Atta way, buddy," Will cheered encouragingly. "Dive *worse*, why don't you? You're looking positively plungiferous."

★ ★ ★

After lunch, on their way to basketball, Zee and Will ambled along under the shady oak trees that lined the path. Zee looked up. The dark green undersides of the leaves only let through a few glimpses of powder-blue sky.

"Now that the octopus is done, and Dead Man's Dive is over, what are we going to do next?" asked Will. "We don't want to have peaked and just fade into boringness."

"Do you mean what pranks can we pull?" grinned Zee. "Well, I'm carving a block with a wolf paw print on it in Arts and Crafts. I figure we can use it to make paw prints in the mud on the lakeshore and lure the guys into following the prints. Then we can have a prize or surprise at the end. No wolf, but maybe a rope swing or something."

"Excellent," said Will. "It'll be a Wolf, Wolf hike. Sort of like a Wolf, Wolf story, only with a happier ending."

"Yeah, good one!" laughed Zee.

"I like your idea," said Will, "but how about a new quest? I really want to find Hidden Falls!"

"Me, too," said Zee.

The boys had heard counselors and old campers talk about the magical hidden spot, but they'd had no luck getting anyone to tell them where it actually was. The tradition required campers to find the place on their own and then never divulge its whereabouts to any other camper.

"Got any idea how to find it?" asked Will. "Last year we looked everywhere. All winter we searched Google Earth. Nothing!"

"Maybe we should just start over," said Zee. "Forget everything we tried and come up with something else. Like, you know, that new guy Kareem? Turns out his brother and even his dad were campers here. Let's go ask Kareem if they told him anything about Hidden Falls."

"No way, man," said Will. "Bad idea. What if Kareem wants to come with us? Hidden Falls is *ours*."

Once again Zee felt scolded, as he had when Will got mad at him for including Skeeter in the pie plan. He shook it off and said, "We'll just ask him for information," he said. "He might be able to help. C'mon. Let's go."

Will sighed, but grudgingly followed Zee to Birch Cabin. They found Kareem there, playing cards with Jim.

"Hey guys," said Jim. "We're just dealing a new game of Crazy Eights. You want in?"

"Maybe another time," said Zee. "We—"

But Will interrupted. "Kareem," he said. "Did your dad or your brother give you the scoop on Hidden Falls?"

"Ha!" said Jim. "Don't be fooled, Kareem. Everybody knows that Will-n-Zee found Hidden Falls last summer, but they don't want us to know that they found it, so they're pretending that they didn't."

"Huh?" asked Kareem.

"Really, Jim, we have no clue where Hidden Falls is," said Zee. "Honest."

"Whaddya say, Kareem?" prompted Will impatiently.

"My brother told me about the tradition of keeping the Falls a secret," said Kareem. "That got me curious, so I bugged my dad about it. All I could get out of him was something about a spring."

"Like a freshwater spring?" Zee asked.

"Yeah," said Kareem. "I figure it feeds into the lake somewhere." He tossed his cards on the bed, saying eagerly, "Let's go look. We could be scientific about it and search every inch of the lakeshore."

"Thanks, Kareem," said Zee. "We—"

But Will socked him in the arm and interrupted him again. "We're going to head out by ourselves," he said firmly. "Just us. But thanks."

"We'd find it in no time with all of us looking," said Kareem. "It'll be awesome!"

The door slammed. Zee and Will were outside before Kareem even finished speaking.

Zee felt like he'd been rude. "Kareem's right, you know," he said to Will. "We'd find it faster with more guys looking."

"This is supposed to be just our thing," said Will. "It'll be our Greatest Triumph Ever. It'll ruin the whole adventure if other people come. No question."

"Okay," Zee shrugged.

"Meanwhile," said Will, "tonight we put teabags in the shower heads. I can't wait for the next person to take a shower—in tea!"

# Chapter Five

But Will and Zee couldn't begin their search for the Falls right away because the next morning, Carlos crowbarred the Birch Cabiners away from the breakfast tables and herded them out of the dining hall and down to the lake. An overcast sky made the water look pearly black as a warm breeze rippled its surface. The boys gathered at the dock in front of the trailer-load of kayaks that had been delivered the day before.

Carlos introduced the boys to their kayaking instructor. "This is Jamie," he said. "She knows everything there is to know about kayaking."

"Morning, campers!" said Jamie. With two hands, Jamie lifted a kayak over her head, then turned and placed it on the boat ramp.

"Morning," answered the boys, some of them speaking around doughnuts in their mouths.

"So," said Jamie. She grinned up at them while she tinkered with the kayak, checking the seat, closing the waterproof hatch, and making sure the yellow paddles had been put together correctly. "Are you ready to become paddlers?"

"You bet! Me first!" said Yasu. "I call the green kayak."

"Dibs on red," said Kareem.

"Whoa," laughed Jamie. "We'll go out paddling for half an hour or so, but before that we have to cover some basics. First of all, everybody grab a life vest."

Zee felt sure he wouldn't need the vest. He could swim. But he got a vest from the rack anyway, because he knew it was a camp rule that you had to wear a life vest anytime you were in a boat. Jamie learned all the boys' names as she fitted each

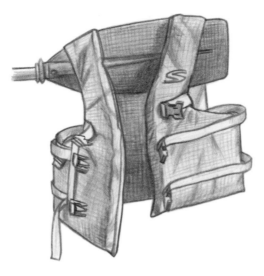

one with a life vest that zipped up to his chin in the front and snapped shut with black plastic clasps. She tugged the side straps to make the vest fit snugly so that it couldn't slip off.

"Okay, now let's move these kayaks over to the put-in. One person at the end of each boat to help carry," said Jamie. As the boys moved each of the hollow, plastic boats closer to the water, Jamie asked, "Who here has paddled before—anybody? Canoe? Kayak? Rowboat? Crew shell? Gondola? Punt?"

"I went canoeing last summer," said Yasu.

"I went bird watching in an inflatable kayak last year with my granddad," said Nate.

"I paddled a rowboat in a pond once," said Vik.

They looked at Zee. "Paddle ball?" joked Zee. "Does that count? That's a kind of paddling, right? How about Ping-Pong? I'm an ace with a Ping-Pong paddle."

"Not quite the same thing," said Jamie, chuckling. "For one thing, the kayak paddle is double-ended. You hold the kayak paddle with your hands about shoulder-width apart." She demonstrated, holding the paddle level in front of her, elbows bent. Then she twisted at the waist to show how to paddle left and then right. "Okay, Yasu. Let's get you in first."

Jamie and Yasu each grabbed one end of the lime-green kayak and lugged it to the water. Jamie made a spinning motion with her pointer finger and they turned the boat around, facing back-ward. "Yep, you go in backward," she said. With his paddle in one hand, Yasu stepped into the cockpit, sat on the seat, and tucked his legs into the hollow space in front of him.

"Piece of cake," Yasu crowed.

"Good," said Jamie. "Easy does it."

The kayak sat with its back end in the rippling water. Jamie bent down and, with one scraping heave, shoved Yasu and his kayak into the water.

"Anchors away!" Yasu yelled. Afloat with the lake at his back, he tried to balance the double-ended paddle across the opening in the cockpit. He squirmed a bit, rocking the boat, and then righted himself.

"Bon voyage!" called Zee, waving exuberantly. "Later, gator."

"Okay, funnyman," said Jamie. "Just for that, you're next." With two hands, Jamie grabbed an apple-red boat and put it in the same position that Yasu's boat had been a minute earlier.

"Aye, aye, captain," said Zee, saluting. He stepped right up and put one foot into the cockpit. Then he reached down to hold on to the side of the boat while he put in his other foot. The kayak wobbled, but he sat down quickly so it didn't tip him out.

"Just slide forward," said Jamie, smiling. She stood above Zee. "You got it."

The rest of the boys launched in quick succession while Zee steadied himself. He quickly learned that if he leaned a little too much to one side, the boat tipped. Too much paddling on the other side, and the kayak veered straight into someone else's boat. *Wham!* Soon, of course, with all the kayaks in the water, there was a cacophony of crashing and splashing and paddles whacking against one another as the boys shouted and cheered.

"Kai-yi-yi-yakkety!" hollered Zee louder than anyone else.

"Settle down, kayakers," said Jamie. "Follow me." She got into her own kayak and then taught the boys to paddle forward, backward, stop, and turn both ways.

It was fun. Zee was sorry when Jamie called out, "Land ho! All ashore that's going ashore," and the boys raced back to the shallow water, climbed

out of their kayaks, and then carried them back to the truck.

"See you tomorrow," said Jamie.

Zee led everyone to lunch, singing:

*Row, row, row your boat,*
*Gently on the lake,*
*Cabin Birchers kayak great.*
*It's a piece of cake.*

# Chapter Six

Later that afternoon, Zee found Will in the wood shop. The room was cool, dark, and dusty, and it smelled of sawdust and turpentine. As Zee's eyes adjusted, he could see the work tables that lined the walls. Woodworking tools hung from a large pegboard. A vice was mounted on the far table where Will was setting his Ping-Pong paddle to dry after gluing the rubber pad back onto the wood.

Will looked up as Zee came in.

"Hey," said Zee.

"Hey," said Will.

Zee felt around on the shelf for the block he was carving to make a life-sized wolf track print.

He had started by sketching a wolf print on the wood, measuring it to be sure that it was the same size as a real wolf print, which a website he'd checked out before coming to camp told him was about four inches across and five inches long. He'd drawn the four paw pads with blunt claws, just like a real wolf's print would look from the bottom, including the pad beneath the toes that was shaped something like an upside-down heart. Then he'd carved around the edge of the sketch so that the print stood out.

"What's your plan for that again?" Will asked, nodding toward the block.

"I'm gonna press it in wet dirt and make wolf tracks to fool people," said Zee. "That's the goal, anyway."

"Good one," said Will approvingly. "This is Camp Wolf Trail, after all!"

"You bet," said Zee.

"So, how was kayaking?" asked Will.

"Good," said Zee. "Everybody liked it."

"Hunh," Will snorted. "Not everybody, because I wasn't there."

"I meant everybody from Birch," said Zee. "We're pumped for our trip. Gotta pass the test first, though, to be allowed to go on the trip."

"Test?" asked Will.

"A kayak test," said Zee. "Pass it oar else. O-A-R. Get it?"

Will smacked his Ping-Pong paddle against his forehead. "Brainstorm!" he said. "I've got a great idea. Don't go on the kayak trip. You've got the perfect out—all you have to do is flub the test and then we can work on finding Hidden Falls while the rest of your cabin is away."

"Flub the test?" repeated Zee.

"Yeah," said Will. "Easy. It's not like you're the king of kayaking or anything, right?"

"No, but—"

"So, bomb the quiz and skip the trip," said Will.

Zee swallowed. He wanted to say, "But I want to go!" He didn't say it, though, and the words stuck like glue in his mouth.

★ ★ ★

For the next two days, Jamie took the Birch Cabiners out in the kayaks to practice. On the second day on the water, she announced it was time for the test.

"It's easy, guys," she said. "You just have to show me that you can paddle forward, backward, stop, and turn both ways. Who wants to go first?"

"Yasu *always* wants to go first," said Nate.

"Can I? Can I?" Yasu paddled forward and showed off his skills. Jamie checked off a list from a clipboard she had stowed in her backpack. After Yasu passed the test, Kareem, Nate, Sean, and Jim did, too.

"You're up, Zee," said Jamie.

Zee wasn't sure what to do. He wanted to go on the trip, but he felt terrible about disappointing Will. It was disloyal. On the other hand, he knew he shouldn't intentionally fail the test. That wouldn't be fair to Jamie; it would be like lying to her and to the rest of the Birch Cabiners.

So Zee followed Jamie's instructions: paddle forward, paddle backward, stop. No sweat.

Then . . .

Jamie told Zee to turn, and in doing so, he rammed into Kareem's boat. *Clonk.*

It was an accident! Really.

"Hey!" yelped Kareem as his boat rocked wildly. Trying to steady it, Kareem whacked the water with his paddle, which sent a wall of water cascading over Jim and Yasu, who splashed Kareem back.

"Splash fight!" somebody shouted. In no time, a full-blown, all-out, take-no-prisoners paddle-splash fight was churning up the lake as though a hurricane had hit. In the end, somehow, Zee landed in the water.

"Anybody else up for a dip?" joked Zee. "Come on in, the water's fine."

Everyone laughed—except Jamie. "Not so fine, Zee," she said. "You have officially failed the test."

"I failed?" said Zee. He pulled his kayak ashore using the tow rope attached to its bow.

"Yeah, solidly," said Jamie. "You can't always be the funny guy. Following instructions counts, and being safe on the water is no joke." She turned to the rest of the boys, who were unusually quiet. "We leave tomorrow, guys," she said. "Pack up tonight. Launch is right after breakfast."

The boys looked at Zee, who for once had nothing to say. Silently, they all paddled their kayaks back to shore and hauled them out of the lake.

"Zee, stick around," Jamie called.

He looked up, his heart pounding under his life vest. "Me?"

"Yes, you."

"See you back up at Birch," said Kareem. Jim gave Zee a sympathetic look, and Nate gave him a gentle wallop on the back, along with a look that said nothing but, *What were you thinking?*

As Zee watched his cabin mates leave, he had a sinking feeling. He'd be truly bummed to miss the overnight kayak trip with the Birch Cabiners, even though that's what Will wanted him to do. Suddenly,

Zee felt rebellious. Why should he miss out on the trip? Who was Will to tell him what to do?

"Hey, Jamie," Zee said. "I'm really sorry."

"I saw what happened out there," said Jamie. "I know you didn't hit Kareem's boat intentionally. But you sure did get into that splash fight intentionally, even though you knew you were still taking the test."

"Yeah," said Zee. "I blew it. But . . . well . . . I mean, do you think you could give me a second chance?"

Jamie tilted her head. "I don't hand out second chances easily," she said. "Give me a good reason why you deserve one."

Zee thought. And as he did, he stared at the kayaks pulled up onto the lakeshore. Their bottoms were sort of scuffed and muddy. Suddenly, Zee grinned. "What if I scrubbed the kayaks and hosed them clean?" he asked.

"Do that and help me load them on the truck and you've got a deal," said Jamie. "Work first. Makeup test after."

"Deal," said Zee. He stuck out his hand to shake, and Jamie slapped a wet sponge into it.

★ ★ ★

Later, wet, tired, and dirty, Zee was on his way back up to Birch Cabin when Max called through the window of the camp office, "Zee! Package!"

Zee ducked into the small room. Max stood and picked up a large package from the floor. "Here you go," said the counselor.

"Thanks, Max," said Zee. He recognized his grandmother's handwriting on the package. He stepped out the door and ran into Will.

"Hey, I heard the good news," said Will. "Excellent work! You threw the test. Now you don't have to go on the kayaking overnight trip. Oooh, what's in the package?" Will grabbed the box.

"About the kayak trip," said Zee, hesitantly. "Actually, I *am* going."

"What? But they said . . ."

"Yeah, I know," said Zee quickly. "I messed up the test. But I actually didn't mean to. I apologized and Jamie gave me a second chance to take the test, and I passed it."

"So, you actually *want* to go?" asked Will. He tossed the box back to Zee, hard.

"Yes, I do," said Zee.

Will frowned. "But we agreed——"

"No," said Zee, firmly and carefully. "I didn't agree. It was your idea that I flub the test and boycott the trip. You came up with that idea all on your own."

"Okay, Zee-row," Will said coldly. "Go yuk it up kay-yukking. I'll find Hidden Falls. And I'll do *that* all on my own, too." Then Will turned on his heel and stalked off.

Zee watched him go, feeling partly mad and partly sad. He sure did wish it had not come to this: a choice between Will and kayaking. If only Will had not been so stubborn! It felt as though Will was gripping their friendship so tightly that he was strangling it. Was this the end of Will-n-Zee?

Just then, Sean came up from behind and jumped on Zee's back. "That's not a care package, is it?" he asked.

"Looks like it," said Zee, grateful for the distraction.

"Is it from your grandmother?" asked Jim, appearing at Zee's elbow with a bunch of other Birch Cabin guys. "I remember your grandmother's package from last year. Cookies, brownies . . ."

"Those little cakes with the filling," added Erik, drooling, "and the gigantic bag of those crunchy cheese things."

"I don't think she sent any of that this year," said Zee. "She's gone all healthy. There's probably broccoli in here."

"Yeah, right," said Yasu. "I'm not letting you or your box out of my sight."

"Me, neither," said Kareem. "You're not lone-wolfing it with that package, my friend."

"We're not letting you scarf it down all by yourself," added Erik. "In fact, I'll carry it for you." Gently, Eric pried the box away from Zee.

Zee had to grin. His buddies from Birch were pretty funny. He was sorry about his fight with Will, but he'd be sorry to ditch the trip with the Birch Cabiners, too. Now, as Eric took the box, Zee said, "Go ahead." He shrugged and held his hands palms up in surrender. "Gram knew you guys would radar in on any treats. She packed enough for us all, I'm sure."

Back at Birch Cabin, Erik sat down with the package. He shook it gently. Then he noticed the neat lettering on the package label. "Master Zenith Doyle," he read. He asked Zee, "Zenith? Your real name is Zenith?"

"It is," admitted Zee, bracing himself to be teased.

But instead, Jim said, "Totally cool. Doesn't *zenith* mean 'the top' or 'the best' or 'the ultimate'?"

"I guess," said Zee. "Something like that."

"You must be named after your grand-mother," said Yasu. "I think she's 'the best' about sending care packages."

"Yeah," said Sean. "It's like she's our Gram, too."

All the campers peered over Erik's shoulder as he opened the box. When they saw what was inside, they were so surprised that they were stunned silent for a second.

"Origami paper?" asked Jim.

"Origami paper," repeated Zee. "Told you Gram was not into sweets anymore."

The smooth squares of colorful paper smelled floral, like a gift shop. Zee was afraid the boys would be disappointed, but Kareem fished into the box and pulled out a pamphlet with instructions for making many different kinds of paper airplanes. "Paper airplanes!" he yelled. "I love making those."

"Let's make 'em, and then fly them in the rec hall after Archery," said Yasu.

"After that," said Zee, "l…" our

favorite S… …ng

…all

"And to give him a hint to make more!" cut in Erik.

"It'll be a Skeeter Fleet Sweet Treat Tree," said Zee.

"Say *that* three times," joked Zack.

"That, that, that," said Zee.

"Good one, Zee-nith," said Jim.

Zee looked down at the fragile plane he was making. He hadn't quite shaken off his disagreement with Will. But even if he didn't feel "the best," he didn't feel like "Zee-row," either, thanks to the guys in his cabin.

# Chapter Seven

The next morning after breakfast, the Birch Cabiners hiked down to the dock where Carlos, Jamie, and Skeeter—closely watched by Cookie—were packing supplies in the dinghy that Jamie would tow across the lake.

"Thanks for the tree full of planes," said Skeeter. "I've never been thanked in such a high-flying way before. I didn't make pies for your trip, but I did pack up some crispy left-over bacon for you to put on your cheeseburgers tonight."

At the word *bacon,* Cookie sat up, tilted his head, and stared intensely at Skeeter.

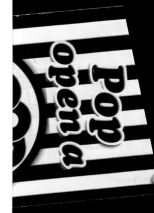

"Cookie, don't give me that look," said Skeeter. "You got your bacon already."

Making the saddest, hungriest face possible, Cookie looked back at the cooler, sighed, sank down, and rested his jaw on his paws.

"Okay, Birch Cabiners," said Jamie. "To your kayaks!" One by one, with quick, smooth heaves, Jamie launched the boys backward into the water.

Zee led the boys singing:

*Row row row your boat,*
*Gently on the lake,*
*Cabin Birchers kayak great,*
*It's a piece of cake.*

As they shoved off, Cookie jumped in the water and splashed around doing a clumsy dog pad-
His long ears floated on the surface of the water
lily pads attached to his
kayaks.

get in the lake without your life vest. You know that."

Cookie didn't seem to care about water safety. It was clear that he just wanted to stick close to his friends—and the bacon Skeeter had packed. But still, as Zee watched, the obedient dog U-turned in the water and paddled back to the shore. Cookie stood next to Skeeter, cast a long face toward the boys in the departing kayaks, lifted his nose to sniff the air one last time, and then shook himself dry, pelting Skeeter with lake water.

★ ★ ★

"Keep your paddles moving, guys," said Jamie. She was in the lead as the group set out across the lake. "Try to paddle quietly. No bubbles, no waves, no wakes, no fancy stuff."

Zee relaxed. It felt great to reach forward, slip the paddle into the water like a knife into soft butter, then p-u-l-l back, using his core muscles against the water's resistance. His smooth forward stroke made his kayak slide through the water with ease. Up ahead, Zee saw Yasu and Erik racing, trying to outdo one another, churning the water white as they plunged their paddles into the water wildly, first one side, then the other. But Zee hung back, thinking, *It's kind of a relief not to be the jokester.* He liked this break from being the guy who pushed the limits all the time, the guy he was when he was part of the trickster duo, Will-n-Zee. And anyway, hadn't he learned the hard way that Jamie was no-nonsense about nonsense?

Sure enough, Jamie called out to Yasu and Erik, "Let's stay together, boys. No showing off. Just smooth sailing, with me in front. I'm *Point*, and you know that means that I'm—"

"Leading the line," all the boys chimed in at once.

held her paddle straight up in the air.
means . . ."

"Don't go any farther."

"You guys are good," said Jamie. "Okay, so if I'm Point, who's Sweep, bringing up the rear?"

"Yo, Sweep, that'd be me," Carlos called from the back of the pack where he paddled along just behind Zee.

After a while, they passed a small island with a bunch of pine trees in the middle of it. Suddenly, Nate shouted out, "Wait!" He grabbed for the small binoculars held on a cord around his neck. "There's a . . . I don't believe this!"

"What?" said Kareem. "What do you see?"

"It's a bald eagle's nest," said Nate, "and it's *occupied.*"

"Where?" the boys shouted and looked, their kayaks bumping into each other as they tried to spin around to see.

"Here, take my binoculars," Nate handed them to Zee.

"How can you be sure it's an eagle's nest?" asked Zee.

"Well, for one I heard the *eep eep eep* sound that eagles make," said Nate. "Two, it's a live tree, and bald eagles only nest in live trees. Three . . ."

Just then, a pair of huge black wings emerged from underneath the green canopy of leaves. As the bird flapped up into the sky, Zee could just make out a bright white head and a yellow beak.

"Awesome," breathed Kareem as the eagle passed overhead, casting its shadow on the water.

"Wow! That was cool," said Yasu. "And we were the first to see it! Wait'll we tell the rest of the guys back at camp."

"Birch Cabin Eagle Spotters," said Erik. "That's us."

They all paddled quietly for a while, think-ing about the eagle, until Vik, who was just behind Jamie, called out, "Land ho! Shallow water!"

"Yeah, thanks for the warning," joked Zack. "I think I'm stuck on a log." He strained to get his kayak moving, laughing as he said, "I am pad-dling forward but going backward!" As soon as he managed to move the kayak forward, a small log bobbed up behind him.

The boys pulled their kayaks up onto the shore and carefully wedged their paddles and life vests inside them. They helped Jamie beach the supply dinghy and carried the bags and boxes to the cleared campsite. When everything had been unloaded and packed in, Carlos said, "Okay, guys. It's time to explore Spikey Island."

Nate, Vik, Zack, and Yasu chose to follow Carlos toward the woods in the center of the island. Jamie led the rest of the boys in a different direction, down to the marshy, muddy shore that ringed the island. Zee, lingering near the back of Jamie's group, watched the guys ahead of him and thought about how wolves travel in a line, stepping in each other's tracks to get through snow swiftly.

*Speaking of wolves*, Zee thought. ...lled his wolf

life-sized paw print on it. He had carved it with a special gouge and then sanded it for hours until his fingers wore through the sandpaper, all the way to the grainy part. Should he use the block, or should he continue his break from trickstering? Zee turned the block over in his hand. He remembered Will saying, "This is Camp Wolf Trail, after all." Remembering made him kind of miss Will; maybe the reason he didn't feel like pulling any tricks was that it wasn't much fun to do them alone. *Yeah,* Zee though, *but it was Will who killed Will-n-Zee, not me. It was Will who'd been all do-it-my-way-or-no-way.*

Out of curiosity, Zee bent down to make a track in the soft dirt. It looked great! So genuine. He wondered how many tracks he'd have to make. One track alone didn't make sense. But a bunch of tracks together could go somewhere, do something, even leave a message behind for someone else to fol-low. The trick was just too good not to do—even if he did have to do it solo. So, Zee went to work making tracks in the muddy swath of shore that cir-cled the island, lagging behind Jamie's group so no

one would see. The shoreline was damp and muddy, which helped. Zee couldn't wait to see what happened when someone spotted the wolf prints.

He could hear the other Birch Cabiners getting farther and farther ahead of him as they were looking for turtles. A mosquito buzzed by his ear. As he moved his hand to slap it, something in the lake back behind him caught his eye.

It was a little dark spot on the flat water. Had *there* a minute ago?

*···g on* the surface? No.

*····· ? Zee*

A dog? It looked like a dog. He squinted. Wait—was that Cookie? How would Cookie have gotten so far out in Evergreen Lake—halfway between the camp dock and the island?

"Cookie?" Zee whispered. Then he yelled the dog's name, "Cookie!" Just then the little head on the water lifted its nose. That's when Zee knew. It *was* Cookie. Why was he in the water? Had he swum all the way from camp? Could he make it to shore?

Cookie seemed to be struggling to stay afloat. Zee didn't know what to do. Frantic, he hollered to the group ahead. "Guys! Jamie! It's Cookie! He needs our help!"

But no one answered. They were too far ahead of Zee to hear his calls. The only reaction to Zee's shout was the sound of the birds, flapping out of the trees at his disruption. Zee's heart raced. Desperately, he tried to think. What should he do? There wasn't time to chase after the group. Cookie needed help *fast*.

Zee's eyes darted to the kayaks pulled up onto the beach. He turned back around and scanned the water, but he couldn't find the little bobbing head on the surface of the water. Maybe the dog had gotten some sense and turned back. Or maybe . . .

From that moment on, Zee felt as if his feet and hands didn't belong to him. He shoved the wolf print block into his pocket, raced to his kayak, flipped it right-side up, slipped his arms through the holes in the life vest, and fastened it tight, hands shaky. *Zip, snap, snap.* He pushed the kayak into the water, hopped in, and fitted his legs in the cockpit, hardly noticing the lurching, splashing, and bobbing as the kayak lunged afloat. Using all his strength, he dug his paddle into the water and strained to move. He could hear a voice—his own, he realized—yelling to the dog, "Hang on, Cookie!"

Zee worked hard. Paddle left. Paddle right. ˙ ˜ Paddle right. The kayak skimmed ˙˜˙ ˙˜˙˙ ˙˜ re of sun-on-

and again he called, "Cookie! Just hang on, boy. I'm coming to get you."

Zee's lungs burned from yelling and from tension and from breathing hard. His arms were numb. He wouldn't let himself think about what would happen if he didn't get to Cookie in time.

All of a sudden, Zee was close enough to see Cookie's eyes, which were wide with fear. The dog locked his gaze on Zee and struggled toward the kayak. Then he slipped under the gurgling, cold water, and all Zee could see were bubbles where Cookie had been.

"*Cookie!*" Zee shouted as loud as he could.

A second later, Cookie surfaced. He whimpered and whined, but valiantly fought toward the kayak, his short legs thrashing the water.

"C'mon Cookie, you can do it!" Zee called. Cookie swam to the side of the kayak. Zee stowed his paddle lengthwise in the cockpit so his hands were free. He reached for Cookie, trying to keep his balance. It wasn't easy. Cookie scrambled and clawed at the hard plastic boat. Zee leaned forward and grabbed the dog's collar. The boat tipped dangerously and rocked wildly from Cookie's weight. Panicked, Cookie clawed at Zee's life vest, shredding the orange fabric cover. Zee's arms began to tremble from the strain. He knew he only had one chance to get the dog onboard before they were both in the water. *I can do this,* he thought.

Zee reached down, grabbed a fistful of loose skin around the dog's neck, and tried to heave Cookie up onto the boat. He had a good hold, but he had leaned too far and . . . *splash.* The kayak tipped and Zee fell into the water on top of the dog. The paddle catapulted out of the boat and knocked Zee in the back of the head. Then the boat flipped over on top of Zee and Cookie and pushed them both under the water.

# Chapter Eight

Cold, dark water closed over his head as if it were solid. Lungs burning, Zee fought his way up and his head burst above the surface. He coughed hard and wiped the water out of his eyes. Zee couldn't see Cookie, though he could feel the scratch of the dog's claws on his shoulders behind him. The weight of Cookie's paws pushed Zee under again. But Cookie was no match for the life vest and Zee bobbed back above the surface of the water. Quickly, Zee turned, flung one arm around the tip of the boat, and grabbed Cookie with the other arm. For a moment, they were face to face in the water, with Cookie's front paws hanging on Zee's shoulders. The dog acted determined to get out of the water.

"It's okay, Cookie. We'll figure this out. Just stay calm, boy," said Zee. But the dog seemed to have an idea of his own. With a great heave, he clawed onto Zee's shoulders and launched himself up and over Zee into the boat. For a moment, Zee was a human ladder. Cookie's burst of force to kick and climb over Zee pushed Zee right back under a third time.

Zee popped up just in time to see Cookie settling himself in the cockpit of the kayak. Cookie's expression had changed from panic to goofy happy. He was a grinning wet mess wriggling on the padded seat, his tongue stretching out a mile. The boat shook from his hundred-mile-per-hour panting.

$\phantom{xxxxxxx}$ to grin. The look in Cookie's eyes

$\phantom{xxxxxxxxx}$ for the

dog and shook his head. "Nice, Cookie," he said. "So why don't you celebrate by howling or something? This'd be a fine time to show off."

Cookie seemed to think that was a great idea. He threw back his head and let out a throaty, *Aroo-oo!*

"Perfect," said Zee. "Good dog, Cookie. Okay, now stay put. Remember, we're in this together." Zee grabbed the rope attached to the front end of the kayak and swam a few feet away to grab the paddle and then toss it back into the kayak. Cookie whined as Zee moved away from the boat. "It's okay, boy," Zee reassured him. "Don't worry. I'm here, and I won't leave you."

Zee actually had no clue how it was going to work out. He was hoping that if he could just swim forward while hanging onto the rope, he could tow the kayak back to the island. As he gathered his strength, they drifted for a moment. Zee let the life vest carry his weight. He tilted his head back and watched the clouds. Where was the sun? Zee could feel a cold current of water running past his feet. His gaze drifted. All he could see was sky, trees, water, water, and more water. Upright again, Zee looked far across the lake to the camp dock. As he scanned the coast far to the left of the distant camp dock, past O'Mannitt's Cove, he noticed something.

White water.

A bubbling stream fed into the lake. Zee knew he'd never seen that stream before. Of course, he'd never looked back at the dock from so far away before, either, or hiked past O'Mannitt's Cove.

*Woof!* Cookie was letting Zee know that he was ready to get back to land. No more resting.

"Okay, Cookie, I hear you," said Zee. He felt calmer now, ready to get going. Zee wound the rope securely around his hand, took a deep breath, and began to swim one-handed back to the island.

concentrating so hard on swimming,

Cookie

side of the boat so that he could lift his head and chest out of the water and look around.

"Hello?" Zee's voice came out softly at first. Then he yelled, "Help! Over here!" Cookie's head popped up as he struggled to stand in the wobbly kayak and bark an S-O-S, *Woof, woof, woof!*

Just then, Zee looked around the bow of the kayak and saw a wonderful sight. It was Kareem, paddling toward him. "Kareem!" Zee hollered. "It's me."

"I'm coming to get you!" shouted Kareem. He paddled so hard that his kayak seemed to fly over the water. "Don't worry!" But in fact, Kareem was going so fast that his kayak collided with Zee's and Kareem capsized himself. He came up sputtering. "Sorry, Zee," Kareem choked out as he righted his kayak. "I got a little excited when I saw you and Cookie. Are you two okay? Man, the water is cold!"

"I know!" said Zee. He felt as though his fingers were frozen around the rope that anchored him to his kayak.

"How come Cookie's in the kayak and you're not?" asked Kareem, hooking an elbow over the side of his kayak to hold on.

"Long story," said Zee. That's when he saw the red and yellow of Carlos's kayak. Behind Carlos were Jamie and all the Birch Cabiners, in a colorful flotilla of kayaks headed straight for them. Relief filled every inch of Zee's body.

"Am I glad to see you guys!" said Carlos.

"Not as glad as we are to see you!" said Zee.

Carlos came alongside the kayak with Cookie in it, took the rope away from Zee, and tied it to his stern. Then Carlos grabbed Zee by the top of his life vest and hoisted him aboard his kayak and into the cockpit. With help from Jamie, Kareem scrambled back into his own kayak.

"Let's go!" commanded Jamie. "Everybody, back to shore. Now."

As they approached Spikey Isalnd, Cookie could hardly stand all the excitement. Fully recharged, he leapt out of the kayak, belly flopping into the shallow water. *Ker-splash.*

"Way to go, Cookie!" cheered Erik. "Plungiferous!" All the kayakers slapped the water with their paddles to applaud Cookie.

There was so much splashing and laughing, they almost didn't hear the urgent whine of the motorboat approaching. "That's going to be Skeeter," Jamie said to Zee. "We radioed for backup when we realized you were out there on the lake."

The motorboat's engine stopped abruptly in the shallow water. Skeeter jumped out of the boat, still wearing his apron from the kitchen. "What happened? Is Cookie okay?" he asked. The wet dog bounded through the water and greeted his owner with splashing enthusiasm, wet paws, and slurpy licks.

"Cookie's fine, thanks to Zee," said Sean. "Zee saved Cookie from

"Thanks, Zee," said Skeeter. "How can I ever repay you?"

Zee grinned. "How about a sky-high pile o' pie?" he suggested.

"You got it," laughed Skeeter. Then, as all the boys pulled their kayaks out of the water and collapsed onto the bank, he continued, "Well, now that I'm here, the least I can do is help make lunch. I've got my apron on and everything!" Everyone laughed, and Cookie punctuated the laughter with a happy, *Aroo-oo!*

"Hey, Cookie, is that how you say *bacon cheeseburger* in dog?" asked Zack.

"Maybe that's why Cookie followed us," said Zee. "He knew we had bacon. Plus, you know dogs are like wolves; they can smell much better than humans. Cookie must have been smelling that bacon all afternoon."

"Wait, I almost forgot!" exclaimed Sean. "Zee, we found a wolf trail."

"What—wolf tracks?" said Zee, pretending to be surprised. It seemed like a year ago that he'd planted those tracks. "So, that means that there are wolves on Spikey Island?"

"No wolves," said Erik. "Just a trickster trying to pull the wool-ff over our eyes, we think."

"Zee! We know it was you who faked those wolf prints," said Jim.

"Who, me?" Zee asked. He dug into the sodden pocket of his swim trunks, pulled out the wood block, and tossed it to Jim. "Think fast," he said. "Hot potato."

Jim snagged the wood block mid-air and looked at the wolf print. He shook his head. "Nice work, wolfman," he said. "Once a jokester, always a jokester, I guess."

"Yeah, man," said Zee.

Jim handed the wood block back to Zee. As he looked at it, Zee knew that Jim was right. He was glad to be back on land—and back to thinking of himself as the jokester. But he also knew that something was missing: Will.

*I bet if Will had been in on this, he'd have figured out a way for the wolf prints to fool the guys for longer,* Zee thought. When he got back to camp, he had two things he must do right away. First, find Will and figure out how they could be friends again, and second, find the source of that white-water stream that fed into the lake, the stream that he had spotted when he was rescuing Cookie. Sometimes at the source of a stream there were *falls*.

Thinking about both Will and the stream cheered Zee up. He balanced the wood block on his wet head and said to the guys, "I'm just getting going with the jokes and tricks, sports fans. So, watch out. You never know what I may think of off the top of my head—my *block* head."

The guys guffawed and Zee thought, *Maybe pretty soon Will-n-Zee will be back in business and there'll be* two *heads at work.* Then Zee smiled. *Or, better still, maybe there'll be a new, improved, multi-headed monster trickster team and* anybody *who wants to be a funnyman can join in. I hope so.*

# Chapter Nine

Camping out on Spikey Island was fun, although everybody was so beat from the Cookie Rescue Adventure that they all conked out just after sunset. They were still pretty ragged the next day as they paddled their kayaks safely and expertly back to camp. The boys dragged their kayaks ashore, sloshed them clean with buckets of lake water, and then loaded them onto the trailer behind Jamie's truck.

"Bye, guys," said Jamie. She waved from the truck window. "It's been real."

"Thanks, Jamie!" the guys hollered as she drove off in the clanky old truck.

The rest of the boys shouldered their gear and headed back to Birch Cabin. But even though Zee was dirty, soggy, sweaty, smelly, sunburned, and had a big bump on his head from where the paddle bonked him, he raced to the wood shop. That's where he figured he'd find Will. Sure enough, Will was there, quietly sanding the edges off a piece of wood.

"Yo," said Zee.

Will looked up from his sanding and raised his eyebrows. "Jeez," he said. "What happened to you? You look like you lost a fight with a crazed mud shark."

Zee grinned. If Will was ragging on him, it was a good sign. It meant Will was back to normal. "Yeah, that's pretty much what happened," he said. "I'll tell you about it later. But listen, I think I _____ ling Hidden Falls."

from Birch or Pawpaw who wants to come along, too. We'd better ask Simon, or some other counselor, to come, too."

"Right," said Zee, relieved that Will had changed his mind about including other guys in the search. Most likely Will had changed his mind about including other guys in *all* of Will-n-Zee's ideas, opening a whole new universe of possibilities for pranks and mayhem, just as Zee had hoped. *Oh man, it's going to be great!* thought Zee as he and Will raced down the trail that led to the cabins.

★ ★ ★

"Watch out below!" hollered Zee at the top of his lungs. He held onto a vine with two hands, ran, and pushed off the bank so that he swung wide out over the water, then let go. *Splash!* He landed in the deep, cool pool at the bottom of Hidden Falls.

The hike to Hidden Falls had not taken long. Zee led the guys from Pawpaw and Birch in the right direction, and they had soon found the spot where the stream gushed into Lake Evergreen. From there, they'd followed the stream uphill. The trail was almost nonexistent, but Kareem and Zack were both really good at detecting trail marks, and Nate helped out with clues he knew from his bird-watching hikes. They *heard* the Falls, but even after they'd hiked up a hill and climbed on to a rock, they saw only the pool down in the ravine. They hiked on, and all of a sudden, around a bend, there it was. Hidden Falls.

"You found it, guys," said Simon. "Well done."

The water crashed down through a series of boulders, pouring over the rocks into a deep pool. Leafy green trees and bushes crowded the Falls from every angle. The dank woods this far back had a ⬚⬚⬚⬚⬚⬚⬚⬚⬚ ⬚⬚⬚⬚ gushing, and in the water. Later, they sat in the shallows enjoying the spray from the waterfall on their faces or lounged on the warm boulders around the pool, turning over rocks, looking for shiny green and blue salamanders. They talked and laughed, forgetting about time. No one thought about leaving. The peaceful current of the soothing, fresh water seemed to hold them in place.

"I could stay here forever," Zee said, leaning his head back against a mossy rock and closing his eyes.

Then Will let loose a bellow that shook the trees. "AAAAAACCCCKKK!"

Zee opened his eyes, bolting upright, but all he could see was a blur of green.

"AAAAAACK!" Will yelled again. "Snakes! In the trees! SNAKES!"

Everyone looked up where Will was pointing. Horrified, they saw that the tree canopy was full of gleaming, lazy, big black snakes looped and stretched out along the branches just above them. Just then, one of the snakes from high up in a tree

startled. It twisted and fell, splashing into the water.

"Run for it!" shouted someone and, in a mess of scrambling, splashing, slipping, and crashing, that's exactly what they did. The boys flew all the way back to camp, screaming and shouting every step of the way.

They never stopped until, breathing heavily, they collapsed in a heap on the grass outside of Birch Cabin.

Sean was the first to catch his breath enough to laugh. "Did you . . ." he gasped. "Did you see when Vik flew straight up into the air?"

"Did you see yourself go from zero to sixty in a split second?"

"Did you see Jim's hair stand on end?"

"Did you see the size of those snakes? They must have been ten feet long!"

"Okay, Hidden Falls," said Zee. "We found you. It was fun, but we're not coming back."

"Right!" said Jim. "Hidden Falls, you can stay hidden."

"Yeah," agreed all the boys.

"No question," said Will.

★ ★ ★

After dinner, a bunch of the boys wandered down to the lake and sat on the edge of the dock. They rinsed their hands and dipped their toes into the clear, green water. Shimmery fish darted around just below the surface. Bugs skittered across the surface of the water making tiny ripples. Max, on waterfront duty, was sitting at the edge of the water, digging his fingers in the sand.

"I've got one word for you people," said Zee.

"Oh no," said Nate. "Here we go."

"Kayak!" shouted Zee. "It's my new word of the day, boys. You know the word *kayak* is a pal-
 ̶ ̶ ̶l̶e̶d̶ the same back and

Zee nodded. "Yeah," he said. "I know."

A group of birds deserted a branch overhead, chattering cheerfully as they took off across the lake.

Max splashed his face with water and stood up. He grabbed the foam rescue tube lying on the ground next to him. The boys watched him, expecting him to raise his whistle to his lips and blow, signaling that they were free to jump in the water. But Max took a deep breath, sprinted past them with a ridiculous smile on his face, grabbed his knees, and launched—foam rescue tube and all—into the water in a massive cannonball that soaked them all.

He quickly came back to the surface, shook out his short hair, and yelled, "Gotcha!"

Wet, laughing, and sliding, the boys raced over to the pegboard with their swimming buddy tags. "Flip your tags!" Vik bellowed.

"Flip your tags, you tag-flipping flag tippers!" Zee yelled. Max climbed out of the water and blew his whistle.

The boys ran to the end of the dock where the water was deep and the lake stretched out, looking endless. One after another, with howls of joy, they plunged in.

# REAL BOYS CAMP STORIES

## Doug Smith

*Doug Smith is working hard "to make the world just a little bit more wild by bringing wolves back to Yellowstone National Park." In this essay, he explains why.*

I was raised on a camp in northern Ohio. My father bought an old farm in the 1930s. When he went to the bank for a loan, they told him the farm had failed. Why would he want to buy such a place? My father said he was not buying the land to farm it. He wanted to start a camp, which had been his dream for most of his life.

The people at the bank thought he was crazy.

But my dad loved nature, and he loved children. He thought, *Why not put the two things together?* He also loved horses and had to get them involved somehow, too. So our camp, Red Raider, had *a lot* of horses. Three barns full of them; nearly one hundred! The rest of the camp was wild, or I thought it was, and because that is where I grew up, I have carried that camp and that wildness in me every day of my life.

When I was a kid, I had plenty of time for exploring. Usually I had a dog with me, and we'd go off to a stream in the woods to look for salamanders and crayfish, and occasionally snakes, frogs, or toads. I wasn't hunting or trying to catch anything; I just liked standing in streams, turning over rocks, watching the creatures, and then putting the rocks back so they could go on with their lives.

hickory, and tulip trees. We looked for birds, too. My dad's favorites were the scarlet tanagers because he loved their red color, and the pileated woodpeckers because of their big red crest and their call. Whenever we heard a woodpecker's call deep in the woods, we'd all stop still—dad, me, and Tractor—and listen.

On those horse rides, we could feel the pulse of nature if we were lucky and patient. If I tried to grab the feeling of being at one with the woods and the animals, it wouldn't come. But if I went into the forest not expecting anything, and just quietly observed, the most beautiful things imaginable would happen. For brief, golden moments I would be one with the natural world.

Today, I study wolves in Yellowstone National Park. Wolves were killed off by people even after Yellowstone became a park because people thought they were bad; wolves were not part of a "civilized" world, so they had to go. But I remember our camp—the salamanders, the crayfish, the trees, the birds, and how I loved it all. To me, camp was wild, not at all civilized, and I thought that to be very good. So I have been part of bringing wolves back to Yellowstone after they were killed off, to make the world just a little more wild, like it was when I was a small boy at my dad's camp.

Growing up at my dad's camp started me on my path toward what I do now, but getting here had many steps along the way. One step was a job studying wolves on a remote island in Lake Superior called Isle Royale.

Wolves intrigued me. When I was a kid, I read as much about them as I could. When I was fifteen, I wrote wolf biologists handwritten letters asking to work with them. No one would hire me because I was too young. But at eighteen, I wrote to all the biologists again, and finally I got lucky and got the job on Isle Royale.

Isle Royale is stunningly beautiful—and stunningly remote. It may be more remote than the far reaches of Alaska, because it sits out in the middle of the largest freshwater lake in the world.

One time, I was sent out alone to track a pack of

at about 11:00 p.m., after resting some and listening to the night sounds, I unzipped my sleeping bag and the bug net on the tent and stood outside in the dark forest and howled. I often tracked wolves by howling for them. If they were around, they'd howl back, and that helped me locate them.

I howled some more, and then some more.

Nothing.

Maybe I wasn't as close to the wolves as I thought I was. Disappointed, I crawled back into the tent and shined the flashlight around so that I could find and swat the mosquitos that had got in.

And then it started.

West of me, several adult wolves wailed a deep, throaty howl. Then, to the east, the pups began to howl.

Uh oh. The adults and the pups were separated and *I was camped between them*. There weren't many ways to get around me; I was on the route to the pups. Had I cut them off—divided the adults from the pups—without meaning to?

Then in the forest I heard something. At first it sounded like the other night sounds, but then I heard sticks cracking and I knew something was coming my way. It was big, and it was more than one animal. I knew it was wolves.

What should I do? Should I crawl out and try to get a look at them? But there was no moon. It was too dark, and also, I didn't want to scare the wolves away. They were coming toward me. They had to have known they were coming toward a person—they can smell their way around in the dark—yet they still kept coming. Normally, wolves are afraid of people, but this pack kept coming closer and closer to me. What were they going to do?

I got out of my sleeping bag and sat as still as I could. Now the wolves were so near that I could hear them sniffing, investigating my camp. They were *right there*, only a few feet in front of my tent! They had come in unafraid. I pressed my face up against the bug net to try and get a look, but it was too dark. I couldn't see them, but I could smell them and hear

Then, minutes later, I heard howling. The adult wolves and the pups were howling at the same time, like a chorus. They had reunited, and they were howling together.

I was overwhelmed. The wolves had come so close to me. They had visited me in my camp and had done nothing more than check me out. I think they had probably heard me howl, and it had made them worried about their pups, so they'd come back from their night hunt early to investigate me and return to their pups. Their visit was as close as I had ever been to a wolf—and in the dead of night! Such an encounter with wolves had never happened to me before—nor has it happened since.

From that time on, I knew I wanted to study wolves. I wanted to find out more about them in order to help them, because so many people hated them. And the feeling that I had when I was alone in the dark with those wolves in the forest? It was the feeling that I had at Camp Red Raider—exploring alone or with my dad—of being connected to nature. I am old now, and I still crave that feeling I got when I was young. It fuels me. For more than twenty years now, I've been bringing gray wolves back into Yellowstone National Park. And it all really started as a young boy in the woods on a camp in Ohio with my dad.

# ALSO AVAILABLE

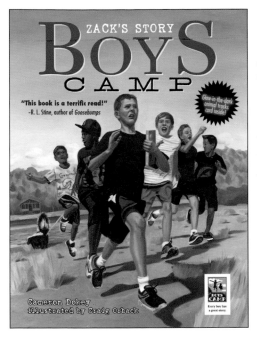

## Boys Camp
### Zack's Story

Written by Cameron Dokey and illustrated by Craig Orback

Being at Camp Wolf Trail is a dream come true for city boy Zack. Finally, he'll have the summer full of challenge, friendship, and *fun* of which he's always dreamed. But nature has surprises in store for Zack: animals, weather, and even the earth itself don't behave the way he expects them to. After Zack makes a mistake that nearly costs him the friendship and trust of his cabinmates, he loses confidence in himself. When a scary catastrophe happens, and Zack is faced with life-threatening danger, will he have the courage and problem-solving smarts to lead his friends to safety?

$9.95 Paperback • ISBN: 978-1-62914-805-2 • ebook ISBN: 978-1-62636-321-2

Sky Pony Press
New York

BOYS CAMP
Every boy has
a great story.

# ALSO AVAILABLE

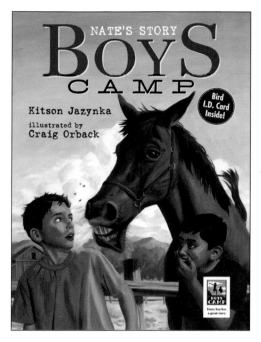

## Boys Camp
### Nate's Story

Written by Kitson Jazynka and illustrated by Craig Orback

Nate has returned to Camp Wolf Trail with a secret: he doesn't want his cabinmates to tease him about his newly found interest in birds. Nate confides in Vik, but can he trust his friend, the cabin jokester? Tension grows when before an overnight horse-riding trip Nate discovers that he has *another* secret. He is terrified of horses, even Herschel, the boney old horse assigned to Nate from the group of rescue horses that the campers ride. Nate shows honesty and bravery when he faces his fears—both of being laughed at for his hobby and of riding horses. But what will Nate do when a wildfire threatens the safety of his friends, the rescue horses, and himself while on a horseback trek deep in the forest? What will be the fate of homely Herschel, the horse no one wants to adopt? And will Nate ever find that owl in the forest?

$9.95 Paperback • ISBN: 978-1-62914-806-9 • ebook ISBN: 978-1-62873-349-5

Sky Pony Press
New York

Every boy has
a great story.